A FUN HALLI

COLORING BOOK FOR

CHILDREN

Copyright 2023
Scoochie & Skiddles, LLC

hello@scoochieandskiddles.com

Visit our website for our
children's story books
www.scoochieandskiddles.com

Made in the USA
Middletown, DE
25 August 2023

36896042R00044